LETTERS FROM THE PACK

OMEGAVERSE HOLIDAY QUICKIES

CLOVER HOLLOWAY

Book Cover: Unfortunate Designs

Independently Published by Unfortunate Productions LLC

Print ISBN: 9979-8-9913742-8-6

BLURB

Daisy thinks she knows who's been sending her letters: the boys that got away. It's been years since they left the small town of Dunning Ridge, and it looks like they're coming back home. Will their declarations of love be enough to convince her to take them back this Valentine's day?

Omegaverse Holiday Quickies are novelettes with more smut than plot. They are meant to be a fun escape with no angst that you can read in one sitting. Have fun and get your spice on!

To everyone who believes in small towns, second chances, and soulmates.

AUTHOR'S NOTE

A note about the Omegaverse Holiday Quickies series. We all love Omegaverse books with lots of character development and conflict resolution, and of course heats, but sometimes you just want a short little palate cleanser to read in between longer novels, or while you're in the waiting room at the doctor's office, or the school pick up line...you catch my drift.

That's where the Omegaverse Holiday Quickies series comes in! I love reading those short instalove/instalust where a OTT man falls hard and fast for a damsel he rescued from the woods/mountain/mafia/ex/etc, but I usually only find them in the contemporary genres. I wanted to capture that same vibe but with an Omegaverse twist.

All of these stories will be of existing packs, or insta-love pack formation, with no angst or third act breakups. They are very short, and meant to be fast, fun, and totally smutty.

They are also light on the Omegaverse pitfalls, and won't always center around a heat. The spice will be spicin' though, I promise you that! If you aren't familiar with Omegaverse, take a look at the short primer I included next.

All my books are queer. The worlds they are set in are queer-normative and there will always be a wide mix of relationship pairings, dynamics, and genders. Even if the primary relationship is a man and a woman, all my characters are pan unless otherwise stated. If that's not something you're comfortable with, my books likely aren't for you.

There are also explicit adult scenes mixed with a healthy dose of kink. Please read the content considerations before diving in.

I really hope you love this series, because I have so many ideas for more holiday quickies!

Stay lucky,

Clover 🍀

WHAT IS OMEGAVERSE?

Omegaverse is a subgenre that takes place in an alternate universe loosely based on canid culture. Similar to wolf shifters, they form packs and have a hierarchy, but there are no shifters in my Omegaverse. There are different *designations* of people - most commonly alpha, beta, and omega. Each Omegaverse may have different designations, rules, and lore depending on the author. In this primer the rules will be specific to the universe I created for these characters, and some details may not be the same as you've read before.

Some things most every Omegaverse has in common though are designations (A/B/O), heats, scents, and knots.

Alphas

Alphas are usually the strongest and most dominant members of society. They are usually big and muscular, and some may have more *alpha power* than others. They can *bark* other designations into submission, forcing them to follow their commands. They also have a special feature at the base of their penises called a *knot*. The knot will swell when the alpha orgasms, and if they are having penetrative sex then it will *lock* them inside their partner. Alphas can be driven into a *rut* when overly aroused.

Alphas are often in positions of power and will behave based on their alpha instincts. Their scents are strong and they will bite a partner to *bond* them.

Betas

Betas are what most people would consider a "regular" person. They are the most common designation in society and aren't as affected by hormones and pheromones. They do not have knots and won't go into a rut.

There are some worlds where betas may be considered less valuable because they are essentially normal humans. In this world, betas are known to be excellent additions to packs because they are level-headed and can balance out the extremes of alphas and omegas.

Omegas

Omegas are usually the rarest and most valued designation in society. Because of their low numbers, one omega may form a pack with several alphas and betas. Omegas are generally submissive and natural caretakers. Omegas have heats where their bodies drive them to breed. They will have insatiable sexual appetites and they may need several partners to satisfy them. If omegas are not knotted during their heat, it can be extremely painful and sometimes dangerous for the omega.

In some worlds, omegas may be considered the lowest rung of society, and even like property. They could be barred from getting jobs or may be otherwise controlled by their families or their alphas. They can be any gender and sometimes assigned male at birth (AMAB) people can get pregnant.

Heats and Ruts

This is a state where omegas and alphas are completely driven by their hormones to copulate. The heat could be on a regular schedule much like a woman's period, or they could be unpredictable. Both options are common tropes in the genre. When in a heat or rut, omegas will often beg for a *bonding bite*, and alphas are driven to *bite* and *claim* their omegas.

These episodes may be controlled by *heat suppressants* or *rut blockers*.

Scent Matches

Scent is super important in Omegaverse. Everyone has some type of scent, everything from sandalwood to strawberry shortcake and more. Alphas and omegas will have the strongest scents, and betas will have milder scents. When someone finds someone with a scent that is utterly irresistible, they are *scent matches*. This is akin to fated mates. Some universes will have different levels of scent matches (scent sympathetic, scent match, soul scent, etc).

Often if there is an incompatible alpha or omega, then they will smell terrible to the main characters. Usually their scents can indicate mood, souring or burning when they are upset, or sweeter when they are aroused. Mates will often *scent mark* each other by rubbing their *scent glands* or cheeks along the other's skin to *claim* each other.

Mates/Bonding

As you read above, scent matches often indicate mates. When an alpha claims a beta or omega, they will bite them to mark them with a *bonding bite*. The bonds will work differently in each universe, but most commonly bonded mates will have a two way mental connection where they can sense each other's moods. Sometimes alphas will force bonds on people who are not their willing mates, and sometimes you have to accept the connection for a bond to stick. Sometimes only the alphas need to make the bite, but sometimes both partners need to claim each other to complete the bond. This is probably the most varied tenet in Omegaverse and it doesn't mean any one is incorrect.

CONTENT CONSIDERATIONS

This is an adult story with explicit sexual content. It's more smut than plot. Like, way more. The characters in this story are polyamorous and have different relationships with each other. That's my nice way of saying everyone is boinking everyone.

In addition to down bad alphas, you will find fingering, penetrative sex, cunnilingus, fellatio, knotting, face fucking, rough sex, unprotected sex, small towns, uhauls, mention of illness (off-page), death of a parent (off-page), love letters, fantasies of anal sex/DP/exhibitionism (off-page), hand jobs, and light hand necklaces.

Hey bug,

Do you remember that day out by the lake? Sure, there were lots of lake days I guess, but I'm talking about a very specific one.

Leo had finally teased you one too many times, and didn't have the size to back up his mouth. Usually, you let it roll off like water on a duck's back, but not that time.

Smitty and I were running late, but we saw you towering over Leo, a look of righteous anger on your face. We stood there watching in shock as you picked him up and tossed him into the lake like he was a moldy bale of hay being tossed in the muck pile. You dusted your hands together for a job well done, and walked off, leaving a sputtering Leo behind.

I think I fell in love with you that day.

1

"It's mail day!" My best friend, Zena, sings out as she waltzes into the kitchen.

I raise a brow. "Z, everyday but Sunday is mail day."

"But today is mail day," she huffs. "Another letter came from your secret admirers!" Zena pulls out a familiar pink envelope with a flourish, dangling it in front of my face. I reach for it, but she pulls it out of reach.

"Nuh uh uh." Zena scolds me, complete with a condescending finger wag. "What do you say?"

I groan. "Oh Zena, mighty warrior omega even if your name is spelled with a z instead of an x," I say the last part under my breath and my best friend glares at me. "Would you be so kind as to let me have my own godsdamn letter—" I lunge with a growl and Zena skitters out of the kitchen. She doesn't get far before I'm tackling her to the couch and pinning her with my larger body so I can wrestle the envelope out of her grip. Sometimes being unusually tall has its advantages.

Zena finally relents, and I emerge victorious with my prize. She sits up with a groan. "I thought you didn't care

1

about these—and I quote—'silly little pranks' from some 'silly little alphas.'"

She's not wrong, I did say that. Back when the letters first started showing up. I was trying to pretend I didn't care in order to protect myself. I thought it was some alphahole playing a prank on the sad, lonely omega who never left her small town and lives in the house she grew up in. I own it now, but still.

But then the letters became personal. Intimate.

Familiar.

They started recalling memories from a past I try to forget. Experiences with boys who left this podunk town to become men. Left me.

"Do you really think it's them?" Zena's question pulls me from my reverie.

"It has to be," I say softly. The memories are written in the way only someone who had been there could. But that's all they are, memories. There are no demands, no questions or declarations of undying love—much to my omega's disappointment.

Rational me knows we should move on, that they aren't coming back. But a small part deep inside can't help but have a little hope.

The letters are all hand written, each with a slightly different voice and vastly different handwriting, and if it is who I think it is, then I know exactly who wrote each one. But there is never a return address on the envelopes. All I can think is one thing: why?

Roses are red
Violets are blue <u>(except they aren't</u>
<u>they're actually purple)</u>
I'm the worst poet
But I still love you.

2

I look at the paper one last time then fold it and shove it in the envelope before I can change my mind. Again.

Austin's the one with the right words. Ever since we were kids. He had an uncanny ability to always say the right thing, especially when it came to Daisy.

All I ever seemed to do was piss her off.

But hoo boy was she gorgeous when she was mad. My little spitfire wasn't one to be trifled with. Loving one moment and as vicious as a hornet the next. Cheeks flushed and fire in her eyes.

Even just thinking about it turns me on, my cock twitching in my jeans. I want to make her pretty skin blush for other reasons. I need that fire to be one of lust and not anger. Well, maybe a little anger is okay. Hate sex can be excellent once in a while.

The loud clang of the uhaul roller door shutting pulls me back to the here and now. Reaching down to adjust my junk, I give an unrepentant smirk to an unimpressed Smitty. "What?" I shrug. "I'm not ashamed of my body, Smitty-boy.

I was thinking about our little flower, I can't help how my dick reacts. He's got a mind of his own."

My pack mate snorts out a laugh, shaking his head at my antics. Smitty and Austin can get so focused on serious shit sometimes. Someone needs to loosen 'em up a little once in a while. It's a role I fill with honor.

Footsteps pound behind me as Austin leaves the house for the last time. Smitty looks at the house, sitting in the bittersweet moment. I'm not gonna let them be all up in their feels for too long, though.

"Goodbye house! Goodbye cracked sidewalk! Goodbye Springfield!" I holler, then head toward the driver's side door of the truck. "It's time to go get our omega! Ow!"

I reach a hand to rub the back of my head where Austin smacked me, shooting my pack lead a glare. "What the hell was that for?"

"You know what it was for," he states matter-of-factly. "And you're not driving. Move."

Fine. I'm not gonna argue. I'll ride bitch for the full thirteen hour drive if it means we get on the road faster. Plus, if I'm in the middle maybe I can tease my pack mates with a little road head to pass the time on the highway. I adjust my cock yet again.

This might be a long ride.

Hi Flower,

I miss you. I've missed you since the day we left Dunning Ridge, if I'm honest. Most of my best memories have you starring front and center. You were my first friend, first love, first... everything. I don't regret chasing our big dreams, because if we didn't at least try we'd always be wondering: what if? I just wish we didn't have to leave you to do it.

But that's life, huh? Full of highs and lows. Decisions you have to make and consequences you have to live with. This time, we choose you, Flower. I don't expect you to have waited for us or anything, but I can't help but hope there's still room in your life for Leo, Austin, and me. Even if it's just as friends.

By now you've probably figured out who the letters are from, and possibly what our next move is. In case you haven't, though... We're finally coming back to Dunning Ridge. Back home.

I can't wait to find out what you've been up to all these years. Can't wait to stare into your deep brown eyes while we relearn each other. Will you let us do that, Daisy girl?

I hope so.

3

"Oh my gods!" I gasp, nearly dropping the letter in shock. Zena rushes over, eyes wide with concern.

"What?! What is it? What happened?" She fusses over me until I clear my head enough to try to explain.

"They're coming home." I mumble.

"Where's your phone? Uh, I'm not sure but we can look for it..." Zena trails off while her eyes skim the room.

"No." I say louder, causing her to look back at me. "They're coming home. To Dunning Ridge."

This time it's Zena's turn to gasp. "Them? Like, *them* them?"

I nod. "*Them* them. Austin, Leo, and Smitty. The letter says they're on their way. Not only that, but they want me back. I think."

Zena snags the letter from my fingers and reads frantically. "Oh my gods." She sounds like my very own mimic. "There's no *I think* about it, Dais. They are coming back *for you*." My best friend tempers her excitement momentarily to ask a cautious question. "How do you feel about this?"

I'm quiet for a few moments while I give real consideration to her question. My heart had leapt into my throat when I first read the news, but how *do* I feel about the boys coming back? I've missed them every single day they've been gone. We didn't part on bad terms. I don't begrudge them chasing their dreams, but I couldn't leave mama to go with them. She needed me here.

After she passed, I guess I could have reached out to them, tried to join their journey. But I was comfortable here. I'm still comfortable here. I find peace of mind in my routine. The regulars at the bakery. Old Mr. Fielding fetching the Sunday paper in his bathrobe—his grandkids get him a new one every Christmas. Gloria from the end of the cul-de-sac walking her poodle, Snooty. So many little moments that stay constant in my life, keeping me grounded. I'm not sure I would have survived city living, even if it was with those boys.

Well, I guess they're men now. I wonder how much they've changed. Did Smitty ever hit that growth spurt he swore was coming any day? Gods, do they still even call him Smitty? His real name is Tristan Smith, but he always insisted it was too fancy a name for a small town boy like himself. Is Austin still lean, or has he filled out in the way of most alphas. He was always handsome, and I can't imagine time being cruel to him. And there's no way Leo still has frosted tips. I hope.

That last thought makes me giggle.

"Penny for your thoughts?" Zena asks, and I realize I haven't given her an answer.

"I think I'm excited," I answer honestly. She doesn't say anything, giving me the space to explain. "I've loved them my whole life, that didn't suddenly disappear when they left. You'd think the loves of my life abandoning me here would have wrecked me, but I was too busy taking care of mama for my heart to break. Then selling my place and moving in here when she left it to me. Taking over the bakery and updating the heck out of it. I've never slowed down enough to fall out of love with them."

Zena hums thoughtfully, but stays quiet, so I continue. "I could hold a grudge and harbor maligned feelings toward them, but why? Is it wrong to want a love that's easy? Does it make me weak not to fight it or make them feel bad about chasing their dreams?"

"Does it matter?" Zena asks, and I look at her in confusion. "Even if someone thinks you're weak for jumping right back in with them, does it matter? Does their opinion matter more than your happiness?"

A smile tips my lips unbidden when I take my friend's words to heart. No, it doesn't matter what other people think about how I live my life or love my partners. And if they judge me? Fuck 'em.

This Valentine's day is shaping up to be the best one of my life.

Hey bug,

I know these other two lugs are writing you letters right now, but I can't wait my turn. Oh yeah, did you notice we were taking turns sending you mail? I didn't want to overwhelm you, and you know how Leo can get. A lot's changed, but that sure hasn't.

Anyway, what we're doing is risky. Trust me, so many people have tried to talk us out of it. But they don't understand. They don't know what we all had between us. We hit our career goals and when we were asked what's next, we all knew it was you.

It's always been you, bug. We can't imagine settling down anywhere but where you are. Be it Seattle, London, or little Dunning Ridge—you're our home.

See you in two shakes of a lamb's tail.

4

The sunlight reflecting off the familiar sign at the outskirts of Dunning Ridge makes it seem like the town is welcoming us with a wink.

"Hallelujah! We fuckin' made it!" Leo shouts just before he plants his lips on mine. I swerve a little in surprise before he launches off me to give Smitty the same treatment. Getting the truck steady again, I huff a laugh at my most excitable pack member. I can't even be mad at him because I think we're all feeling the same joy right now.

We're home. Well, almost. It won't feel like home until I've laid eyes on my bug.

"We're goin' straight there right, Aust? Please tell me we're going straight to Daisy's house. I can't wait any longer," Leo pleads. We should probably go to our rental first, maybe take a shower to clean off the road funk before we see our girl for the first time in years. But I think my pack mates may riot if we detour for any reason. To be honest, I don't want to wait either.

One look at Leo and I know I can't tease him any longer. Even if he does deserve it after the *activities* he and

Smitty partook in while I was stuck behind the wheel with a hard on. Insatiable, those two.

"Yeah, baby. We're going straight there." I smile at the unfettered joy coming from Leo's side of the bond. When we left Dunning Ridge, none of us were together romantically. We had some encounters with Daisy—even together as a kinda pack—but while we've been gone, our pack bonds solidified and a new kind of love grew between all of us. I wonder what Daisy will think of that development. Will she accept it? Reject it? Knowing my sweet bug, I can't imagine her thinking twice about the fact we all fuck each other now, but there's always a chance.

Only one way to find out.

The town looks more or less the same as when we left. Same shops on main street, though the bakery looks as if it's gotten some upgrades. Pink and red hearts adorn the lamp posts, and shop windows display Valentine's treats and gifts. It's like Hallmark threw up everywhere, and I wouldn't have it any other way.

The truck bounces as I steer out of downtown onto the more sparse side streets. The streets aren't paved as smoothly out here, and they eventually give way to dirt roads and gravel driveways. That's where our girl lives, in the house she grew up in. We may not have been back, but we still have some friends who never left Dunning Ridge, and sometimes we just couldn't help asking for a little update on Daisy. We're weak when it comes to our omega.

The excitement in the truck reaches a fever pitch when Daisy's home comes into view. The craftsman style house looms ahead like a beacon of hope and love. Painted a soft sage green with a white wraparound porch, it looks cozy and homey.

Daisy must have heard the truck coming because the

front door whips open, the screen door slamming aside a moment later. Then she's there. Our omega. Even more beautiful than I remember.

She stands at the top of the porch stairs, one hand on the railing, the other covering her mouth in surprise. Her long black hair has been left loose and it blows in the breeze. She's wearing the sweetest white dress, a ribbon accentuating her waist. A present I desperately want to open.

I slam the truck into park and shut off the engine, dousing the cab in sudden silence. We're all stunned, it seems. Too engrossed in seeing our bug again to move or speak. Smitty gets it together first, jolting to open the cab, nearly falling out the door in his haste. Leo and I aren't far behind. We round the hood and approach the porch with caution, stopping when we're a few paces from the wooden steps. We don't want to overwhelm her and aren't sure what her reaction will be. Good or bad.

Then the breeze shifts direction and brings with it the sweet scent of honeysuckle and apricot. It nearly brings me to my knees. My pack mates aren't unaffected, either. Smitty takes a step forward as if he's no longer in control of his actions. Leo lets out a soft moan and begins a stuttering purr. My mind narrows on a single truth.

She's our scent match.

Daisy girl,

You know I've never been good at writing. The C I got in every English class during high school sure proved that. Austin keeps telling me the words I write don't matter so much as the feelings I get across. So, I guess here goes...

No matter how many days we've been gone, my love for you has never faded. It burns in my chest, keeping my soul warm. The closer we come to making it back to you, the larger the flame grows. It'll be an inferno by the time you're back in my arms, and all I can say is burn, baby, burn.

Memories of your smile have kept me sustained on even my saddest days. Even if you never take us back, one point I held you as mine so I can be sure I know what true happiness feels like.

And that feisty attitude of yours, well... that makes my cock hard.

Sorry not sorry, Daisy girl. There's no world I believe in where we aren't together, so you're stuck with me and my obsession.

5

S cent matches.

There's no mistaking it. I've never felt so drawn to a scent before. Never felt so happy, so... horny.

Seeing them is a shock to my system. I'd heard their truck come up my drive. I also may have been staring out the window hoping today would be the day. It's Valentine's day, and even though it's an over-commercialized holiday, there's a small part of me that thinks it's romantic they showed up on a day meant to celebrate love.

Three of the handsomest men I've ever laid eyes on get out of the uhaul and stand before me. I don't have time to take them in fully before the breeze steals my breath away, assaulting my senses with smells. Cinnamon and tart apple with a hint of caramel. Warm vanilla and bourbon. Sugary sweetness to round it all out.

I don't know which scent belongs to which alpha, but what I do know is they're *mine*. By the looks on their faces, they've realized I'm theirs, too.

In truth, I've always been theirs. They left before I presented, and I've always been curious what their scents were, but nothing in my imagination compares to the all encompassing effect they're having on me right now.

Finally, I push the fog from my mind so I can truly look at the men before me.

Like I guessed, Leo no longer has frosted tips—thank gods—but he has added some new ink. The designs disappear under his shirt, and I want to see what else is hiding under there. His eyes are alight with need and joy as he stares at me, his entire body pulled taut as if he's poised to tackle me at any moment.

Smitty's no longer the lean boy I remember. He's grown at least four inches, bringing him close to Austin's height now. His shoulders are broad and a sexy scruff covers his jaw. His azure eyes connect with mine, and I'm lost in them until he gives me a wicked smirk. I break eye contact as my cheeks flush with heat. Whether it's from embarrassment or desire, I'm not quite sure. It's then I notice his fingers are intertwined with Leo's. Are they together? That's new. And not at all unwelcome.

"Bug." The old nickname is rasped out, laden with so much emotion. Austin. My bear. He was always my rock in any storm. A gentle giant with so much love in his heart. Seeing him again kicks my body into gear. Before I know it, I'm flying down the steps and into his arms. He swoops me up without hesitation, lifting me and spinning around with me tight against his chest. His face burrows against my neck as he takes a deep inhale of my perfume, a purr immediately rattling against me.

"Bug. Baby. Fuck. I missed you so much. We missed you so much." His words are muffled against my skin, but I hear them all the same. When I don't respond, he pulls back to search my face. He furrows his brows in concern and

22

puts me down, hands flying to my cheeks to wipe away the wetness there. I hadn't even realized I was crying.

"Daisy. Fuck, why are you crying? I'm sorry. I shouldn't have grabbed you. I didn't mean—"

I grip his shirt and pull him back to me, cutting off his panicked apology with a fierce kiss. Austin freezes for a moment, then relaxes against me, returning my affection. Warm vanilla and bourbon hit me, identifying the owner of at least one of the delicious scents I first smelled when they arrived. He licks the seam of my lips and I open so he can sweep his tongue to tangle with mine. I hear twin groans when a burst of my perfume surrounds us.

I've always felt like Austin, Leo, and Smitty were mine —even before I could scent them. Before I knew they'd designated as alphas and I, an omega. The fact they're my matches just makes sense. Like I told Zena, why fight fate? Why fight happiness? I don't want to.

We break our fevered kissing and Austin rests his forehead against mine. "You're mine," I breathe out.

Austin nods against me. "Yes. We're yours. Always yours. And you're..." He trails off, body tense and a question in his eyes as he pulls back.

"I'm yours," I agree, and the tension leeches from his frame in an instant. Then I'm surrounded, two more hard bodies pressing against me, dropping kisses and scent marking wherever they can reach.

Suddenly, I need them with the fire of a thousand suns. I need to feel them against my body. I want to feel their knots for the first time. I want their teeth in my neck. And I want it all now.

6

I'm not sure what I was expecting when we reunited with Daisy, but it wasn't her immediately trying to jump our bones. Not that I'm complaining.

Her sweet honeysuckle and apricot scent blooms brighter with her arousal and it snaps something in me. I squat a little, grip under her thighs, and haul her up to me. Her legs automatically wrap around my waist and she pushes her sex against my rock hard cock through my jeans. Her panties are so soaked already I can feel it through multiple layers of material and I groan as I walk up the porch steps. Refusing to let go of my omega, I growl in the general direction of my pack mates and one of them rushes to pull open the screen door for us. I'm not entirely sure who it is since my focus is entirely on my sweet flower in my arms.

Doesn't matter. All that matters is getting this woman somewhere soft so we can claim her. We enter her home and I pull up short in the foyer, unsure where to go. Somewhere in the back of my subconscious is the desire to explore my mate's home, to examine all the personal touches she's put into it. But my alpha hindbrain is in charge right now, so all that will have to wait.

Daisy is still nuzzled into my throat, grinding against me, so I slide one hand up her spine and into her hair to pull her back to make her look at me. "Where to, flower? Are you gonna invite us into your nest?"

She squirms and whines. "Yes, please. Nest. Upstairs. Need you."

We're moving fast but I'm not about to look a gift horse in the mouth. We aren't just scent matches, and Daisy isn't just the girl we've always loved. She's our destiny. We were an inevitability. And I'm not about to question fate.

Locking her back against me, I traverse the stairs two steps at a time, eager to get to her nest. It's easy to find, her scent emanates the strongest from behind a door at the end of the hall. Unwilling to wait for Austin or Leo, I shoulder the door open and step into the omega suite. Daisy wiggles, trying to get down, so I place her gently on her feet. She dives into the sunken area in the middle of the room and starts pushing blankets and pillows around frantically.

She's nesting. Our omega is building a nest for *us*. That's a heady feeling, one I can tell my pack mates recognize as well based on the emotions radiating down our bonds.

Even if Daisy technically asked us to come into her nest, we know better than to enter it before she's done arranging it to her liking and she formally invites us in. Taking my eyes off my pretty omega, I take in other details in the room. Large windows line one wall, covered by sheer curtains to temper some of the light coming in. On the opposite wall is a door that looks like it may lead to an en suite—something very important during an omega's heat. The copious amounts of sweat and cum can get to be a little much sometimes. Or so we've been told. We've never been with anyone else, and never seen anyone through a heat. We've never felt a connection with anyone the way we have with Daisy.

Small hands tug on my shirt. I didn't even realize Daisy had gotten up, but she's here now, whining and attempting to pull my clothing off. Does she want it for her nest? Gods I hope so. I whip my shirt off eagerly, contentedly surrendering it to my pretty flower. She buries her face in it, inhaling my scent, then does the same to Austin and Leo. My pack mates stare at her in awe as they comply with our tiny omega's demands.

She hums happily and returns to her nest with her bounty, strategically weaving our shirts in with the pillows and blankets according to a plan only her instincts know. It's beautiful to watch. When she's satisfied, she kneels in the center and looks at us.

"Alphas," she whines, "Austin, Leo, Smitty, come here. Please."

"May we enter your nest, omega?" Austin asks.

"Yes, please." Daisy's official permission spurs all three of us into action and we kick off our shoes and socks by the door before joining our omega in the center of her nest, careful not to disturb the walls she's built. Even Leo, who's like an excitable puppy most of the time, treats her nest with a reverence I've never seen from him before.

Austin is our pack lead, so we defer to him to make the next move. He doesn't hesitate, knee walking to our omega and pulling her against him while he kisses the hell out of her. He urges her to lay down and she complies, Austin holding his weight over Daisy so he doesn't crush her while they continue assaulting each other with lips, teeth, and tongues.

My cock is rock hard, pressing painfully against the

zipper of my jeans, when I feel Leo press against my back. His lips reach my ear as his hand slides around my torso, creeping toward my waistband.

"Fuck. That's hot isn't it? Can you believe she's so perfect, so willing to have us without question?" His fingers deftly undo the button and zipper, then dive under my briefs to grip my shaft. I suck in a breath, my eyes never leaving Daisy and Austin. His summery scent of bomb pop popsicles hits me next. Leo strokes my cock and bites my shoulder, then whispers in my ear again, albeit loud enough for the others to hear. "Do you think our Daisy girl would care if we play? Maybe she'd want to watch?"

Daisy's head snaps toward us, her eyes zeroing in on my crotch where Leo has pulled me out to get a better grip. She licks her lips when she notices the metal glinting on my cockhead. My apadravya piercing. Leo's hand knocks into it on his next stroke and my hips involuntarily thrust forward. She's not saying anything, but the heat in her eyes is unmistakable.

"What do you think, bug?" Austin asks her softly between nips to her skin. "Are you okay with the fact we're all intimate with each other? That we all fuck? We've never been with another omega—no one outside the pack since we left you."

I wait for her answer, a little nervous about how she'll react. I needn't have worried, though. Our Daisy girl nods and bites her lip. "I want to watch."

All three of us groan in unison at how utterly perfect our mate is.

7

Daisy

My body is on fire in the best way. My boys came back to me, and I need them. It's so hot in here, and my clothes start to feel very uncomfortable. My clit throbs, begging for attention, and slick drips out of me at an alarming rate. It almost feels like the beginning of my heat, but that can't be right. I've never been on suppressants or anything, but my heats come every three months like clockwork. I'm not due for another three weeks.

Then again, I have heard stories of true scent matches and bonding bites kickstarting an omega's heat, so I guess it isn't unfathomable that may be what's happening right now. Especially with Austin's warm vanilla and bourbon making my omega purr.

I want to keep watching Leo and Smitty touch each other while Austin licks my skin, but I need my clothing off. Ripping my gaze away reluctantly, I whine and tug at my clothing, trying to rip it away. Austin notices.

"Do you want this pretty dress off, bug?"

I'm nodding my agreement before he even finishes his question. A low purr vibrates his chest and he sits up on his knees, pulling me along with him. He crashes his lips to mine as his hands wander down my body. When he reaches the hem of my dress along my thighs, he doesn't hesitate to grab two fistfuls of the fabric and slowly drag it up my frame. My breaths saw in and out like I've run a marathon, but Austin doesn't stop kissing me until the last moment when he has to break our connection to pull my dress over my head.

I'm not wearing a bra, and all three alphas growl when they see my bare breasts for the first time. Austin wastes no time ducking his head to pull one of my already taut nipples into his mouth, licking and sucking while he palms my other breast.

"Fuck! Austin!" I cry out at the onslaught of pleasure.

Heat of another body nears my back and tendrils of cinnamon, apple, and caramel tingle my nose. Suddenly my head is roughly tilted back by my hair, and my eyes meet Smitty's just before his mouth crashes to mine. He urges me to lean against him, so I do as Austin licks and sucks his way down my body. When a hot mouth reaches the apex of my thighs, my hips buck in anticipation.

"Mmm, little flower, do you want your alpha to taste you?" Smitty purrs. It's a rhetorical question because as soon as he asks it, my panties are ripped away and Austin's hot tongue dives between my folds. Smitty releases his grip on my hair in favor of running his palms up my torso to grab my tits, and I look back between my legs, watching Austin devour my pussy like it's his last meal.

Before the boys left, we'd fooled around and lost our v-cards to each other, but the awkward yet passionate fumbling of back then is nothing compared to the finesse my body is being worked with now. Smitty pinches my nipples and I fall over that edge with a scream. Austin never lets up between my thighs, working me toward another orgasm before I can even come down from the first. My clit is sensitive and my hips wiggle, trying to get away from the pressure, but Austin places a heavy hand on my pelvis just below my tummy to hold me in place.

Two thick fingers spear into my core. "One more, omega. I need another on my tongue," the alpha between my thighs growls before he latches his mouth to my clit once more. He circles the sensitive bundle of nerves with the point of his tongue, teasing me with indirect pressure. All the while he pumps his fingers in and out of me, rubbing that sweet spot on my upper wall each time. My pussy clenches around him, wanting more. He presses harder on my pelvis at the same time he sucks my clit hard. I detonate, my slick squirting all over Austin's face and my scream filling the room. He groans and licks up every drop.

Smitty is still behind me, now lightly running his hands over my body as I come down from my high, my thighs trembling from my release. Austin gets up to his knees once more, and turns to Leo who's moved and is now next to him. "Want a taste?"

"Fuck yeah!" Leo doesn't hesitate, just grips the back of Austin's neck and clashes their mouths together. Leo licks into the other alpha's mouth in search of my flavor, moaning each time he gets a hit of it.

They pull apart, both breathing heavily, then Leo looks at me with a lascivious grin.

"My turn."

8

One hit of my omega's honeysuckle and apricot flavor and I'm done for. I need her more than I need air. I've never claimed to have strong willpower, and I'm not about to start now.

Austin barely moves out of the way before I launch myself at our omega, covering her body but careful not to hurt her. My hands grip her breasts while my lips meet hers. She gives as good as she gets, my perfect match in every way.

I drag my mouth to her neck, biting near her scent gland but not quite breaking skin. She bucks under me and my needy cock weeps precum in my boxers. I want to draw this out, to savor it, but I can't. I bite her lobe then growl into her ear. "Present for me, omega."

A shudder ripples through her body before she goes to roll over. I sit up to strip out of my pants and underwear as swiftly as possible, my eyes never leaving my omega as I watch her get into position. Fuck me. That's so fucking hot.

Smitty's still behind her, so this new position puts her head in his lap, right in front of his hard cock I'd pulled out earlier. She licks her lips and stares up at my pack mate. He rumbles a purr and grips the base of his cock, holding it out like an offering to our goddess omega mate, his piercing glinting in the low light. "It's all yours, flower. Take what you need," he encourages.

Laughing, I slide into place behind Daisy, notching my ruddy cockhead at her dripping entrance. "Well, as long as you share with me sometimes, too, Daisy girl," I add playfully, then thrust my hips forward and slam home.

I nearly come immediately. I wouldn't have been embarrassed if I did, but I have a deep need to get my mate off on my cock before I fill her with my cum. I try thinking of unsexy things like when we had to express our old dog's anal glands or my grandmother's giant mole—the one with the hair growing out from the middle.

But then Daisy makes a wet sound as she chokes on Smitty's cock and it's no use. I just have to work faster to get her off before I end up a two-pump chump. Smitty's head is thrown back in ecstasy, eyes closed, one hand behind him supporting him and the other wrapped in her hair, guiding her up and down his shaft. I stop my thrusts and angle her hips upward a little, then slam back into her tight pussy, hitting her g-spot. She cries out around Smitty's dick before pulling her mouth from his cock to beg. "Yes! Fuck! There, alpha! More!"

Who am I to deny my mate? My grip on her hips tightens to the point I know I'll leave little bruises, evidence of my claiming. My alpha preens, satisfied our mark will grace our omega's body, even if it isn't a bite.

Her skin is hot under my hands, a sheen of sweat glistening on her skin. My knot teases her entrance on every thrust, and I know I won't last much longer. I pull out of her, causing her to cry out, but she isn't left empty long.

Needing to see her face when I come in her the first time, I flip her over and push her ankles over my shoulders, then fuck my cock back into her wet heat. Banding an arm around her shins to keep her in place, my other hand snakes between us to rub furiously at her clit. Her greedy cunt clenches around me and I know she's close. Thank fuck.

Her head is thrashing in Smitty's lap while he strokes his cock, and just as I feel her walls flutter around my shaft she locks eyes with me and says something that nearly makes my heart stop.

"Bite! Please, Alpha. Claim me!"

I pause my thrusts and she glares at me. "Are you sure Daisy girl? I won't survive it if you aren't sure and regret it later."

Her gaze softens. "Yes, Leo. Please. We've waited so long."

Like I said, I've never claimed to have strong willpower, and it certainly isn't going to magically kick in when my omega is asking me to claim her. I lean forward, covering her body with mine and pushing her knees to her chest. My thrusts become punishing, the angle changed, and she cries out in pleasure.

My knot pushes past her entrance to settle in that special spot omegas have, and my teeth find her neck. I bite down, claiming her as mine as she comes on my knot, following her immediately over the cliff and filling her with my spend. I unlatch my teeth and lick over my mark to tend it when Daisy lunges forward and viciously bites the spot where my neck meets my shoulder. I roar as the bond snaps into place, her pussy milking me for every last drop of cum.

Locked in my omega, I bask in the love and content flowing across our new bond, finally feeling whole.

9

Austin

oly Fuck. Leo and Daisy just bonded each other. There's an echo of our omega down the bond I have with Leo, and I'm relieved to find no regret or anger coming from her. She's truly ours now, and seems happy to be so.

Leo's is purring louder than a jet engine and there's a sense of calm radiating from him I've never felt before. Daisy girl's what we've always needed.

And now she's ours. *Mine.*

Well, she will be once we bond. I can't wait to sink my teeth into her soft skin. Assuming she lets me of course. I won't do anything without her consent, no matter how badly I may want her.

Daisy's eyes open sleepily and she looks toward me. Her perfume blooms, filling the nest with even more honeysuckle and apricot, before she holds out a hand. "Alpha. Need to taste you."

Leo's knot hasn't gone down, but that's not going to stop me from giving my omega whatever she wants. It isn't like we haven't been that close before. I crawl to them and settle next to her head, stroking a lock of sweaty hair back from her forehead. She leans in an attempt to get to my dick, but her movement must tug on Leo's knot because they both groan. I gently push her back until she's lying flat once more.

"Do you trust me?" I ask her, and she nods immediately. Careful not to jostle her or kick Leo in the face, I swing a leg over her to straddle her chest, settling my knees in the soft bedding on either side. "One day I'm gonna fuck these pretty tits, bug, but I want to feel your hot mouth right now."

She eagerly nods again and drops open her jaw, sticking out and flattening her tongue in anticipation.

I groan at the sight. "Oh, fuck, bug. Such a good fucking omega for me."

Shifting up her body, I slap the head of my cock on her waiting tongue before pushing into her mouth. I move slow, watching her closely for any sign of discomfort, but she takes at least half my length before she gags when I hit the back of her throat. I go to pull back, but my naughty omega's hands fly up to grip my ass, urging me for more.

"Do you want your alpha to fuck your face, little flower?" Smitty asks, cock in hand as he slowly strokes himself.

Daisy moans and nods her head as best she can with my cock in her mouth. "Fuck, you're perfect, bug."

Smitty moves out of my way and I lean forward, bracing my weight on my elbows above her head so I can thrust deeper into her throat. She can take more of me at this angle, and she swallows another inch on each thrust as her throat starts to relax until I'm buried so deep her lips kiss my partially swollen knot.

"Holy fuck, Daisy girl. You took all of him," Leo says in awe. "I can't do that and you can bet I've tried."

I'm too lost in my girl to rib him, pulling my hips back and thrusting in again until I'm fucking her face in earnest. My abs are tight and I'm glad Smitty forces us to do all those planks at the gym. I'll never complain again if it's prepared me for this.

Daisy takes me like a champ, eyes watering, dripping saliva down her cheeks and chin, her tongue pressing along the bottom of my cock. The most beautiful mess I've ever seen. Suddenly she bucks under me and moans around my shaft, nearly making me come. I glance backward under my arm and realize Leo's knot must have deflated, because Smitty has his face between her thighs, cleaning her with his tongue.

Leo makes his way around to the top of the bed, kneeling in front of me to watch our omega swallow my cock. He smirks, then reaches under me to fondle my balls. I jerk forward with a shout, then pull my shaft from Daisy's mouth, growling at Leo. "You brat."

"Just keeping you on your toes, alpha," he teases. Quick as lightning, I dismount my omega's chest and tackle Leo to the floor, manhandling him to his stomach before I lay my weight along his back, pinning him with my cock nestled in the crack of his ass. I trap his wrists in hands and growl in his ear. "You want to play this game when we finally have our Daisy girl between us? You think I won't put you in your place while she watches?" I chuckle darkly. "Now watch as Smitty claims our omega. Without being able to touch yourself for any relief. You'll have to sit here with an aching cock, feeling her pleasure through your new bond, without doing a single thing about it."

While I've been subduing the bratty alpha beneath me, Smitty's shifted so he's thrusting into our bug from behind while she's on her hands and knees. His hand is shoved under her, between her thighs, obviously playing with her clit while he fucks her hard. Leo whimpers when he sees Daisy staring at him, likely regretting his choice to play with me.

Shifting to hold both his wrists in one hand, I shove my hand under us both until I can grip Leo's cock. "Seeing our girl get wrung out is putting me in a generous mood, so I'll let you come." Leo sighs in relief until he hears my next words. "But not until she comes at least twice. So you better hope Smitty's feeling generous, too."

10

I don't really care if Leo gets to come or not, but I do care that my omega comes multiple times on my cock before I knot her, so he got lucky today.

Redoubling my efforts, pinch my little flower's clit and hold it while I fuck right into her g-spot. She's got to be feeling my piercing dragging against it the way her pussy is strangling my cock each time I sink into her. She whines and squirms, trying to get my fingers where she wants them, but I keep holding tight a little longer.

After a few more strokes, I slam in hard and release her clit. She screams as the little bud fills with blood the overwhelming sensation making her come. My little flower might like to play with clamps if her reaction is any indication. Her pussy gets so tight it's hard for me to keep thrusting until she rides out her orgasm. Slick drips down my balls and along her thighs, the squelching sounds of our sex obscene.

Daisy starts to go limp beneath me, her arms too shaky to hold herself up any longer. I lift her until her back is to my chest, never stopping my movements. My hand snakes between her breasts until my palm settles lightly against her throat, and she rests her head on my shoulder. "Bite, please, alpha. Bite me."

My heart swells with unadulterated joy. "Not yet, flower. Give me one more. I want you to come on my cock one more time before I knot you and claim you as mine forever." Her head tilts to the side, offering her submission, and I nearly cave to the temptation to sink my teeth into her early.

"Leo. Go help get our omega off and you can make yourself come." Austin infuses a little alpha bark into his command and Leo scrambles to obey. Not that I think the bark was needed, but our pack lead knows the bratty alpha enjoys it. Leo throws himself to the bed and shimmies back until he's positioned between Daisy's thighs. He spreads her pussy lips with his fingers before licking from her hole where I'm stretching her, up to her clit.

"Oh! Gods, Leo! Fuck!" Daisy cries as Leo assaults her with his tongue.

I tighten my hold on her throat a little and growl in her ear. "If you're going to scream anyone's name while I'm inside you, it's gonna be mine."

In truth, I don't care if she screams my pack mates' names in the throes of passion, but because I haven't claimed her yet my alpha is feeling a little extra possessive. I scrape my teeth along her pulse point and she whimpers. "Yes, alpha." I nip her ear in warning. "Y-yes, Tristan."

Hearing my omega call me by my real name and not my nickname makes me nearly feral. I've never liked my given name, always feeling it was too formal. But coming from her lips it makes me feel seen, wanted.

"Mmmm fuck yes, flower. I want to hear you scream my name or alpha whenever I make you come from now on.

Starting. Right. Now!" I punctuate my last three words with hard thrusts until my knot slips into her pussy and I sink my teeth into her skin. She screams my name as she comes on my knot. I give her my arm and she takes hold of it greedily, bringing it to her mouth so she can bite me right back. The bond clicks into place and then it's my turn to scream her name as I see stars and fill her with my cum.

11

Daisy

Smitty's knot finally releases me and he slips from my body, a torrent of cum dripping out after it. I'll gladly call him Tristan in bed—because let's be honest, it isn't sexy to yell Smitty out during a heated moment—but my brain will always call him by his nickname otherwise. It's how I've always known him, and even though I love what Tristan can do to my body, I don't want to give up the boy I once knew who never gave up on us.

My pussy is sore and I'm feeling well-fucked, but there's still one thing missing.

Austin pulls me into his lap gently, encouraging me to bury my head in his neck as he does the same to me. He rocks me slowly side to side as I catch my breath, before he mumbles against my skin. "How are you feeling, bug? We can wait if it's too much. I don't want to hurt you."

Oh my big, sweet, giant. Instead of answering with words, I lift to my knees until his hard cock notches at my entrance and sheathe him completely in one slow stroke. We both groan as he bottoms out, and for a few moments we just sit there in silence, his cock nestled in my pussy while our hearts beat in sync.

"I love you Daisy. So fucking much," he rasps against my skin. I pull back so I can move my lips over his. Slow and sweet this time, I try to imbue all the big emotions I'm feeling into the kiss. When we drift apart, I stare into his emerald eyes before I answer his confession with one of my own.

"I love you, too, Austin. I think I always have." Glancing to my two bonded alphas—whew that's crazy to say—I push love down our connections. "And I love you, Leo. Smi–I mean Tristan." I scrunch my nose. "Okay that's gonna take some getting used to."

The alpha in question laughs softly. "You can call me anything you want, flower, as long as you call me yours. I love you endlessly, Daisy."

I look at Leo, feeling his need through the bond. "I love you so big, Daisy girl." I grin at his phrasing. So simple, but so meaningful. He used to tell me that when we were kids. *I love you so big.* It's so perfectly *us.*

I turn back to the alpha holding me. He's been so patient, waiting for me to be ready, but now it's time. "Make me yours, Austin."

He purrs, laying back in the nest and bringing me with him so I'm on top. "Ride me, bug. You own my body and soul. Make me *yours.*"

Our joining isn't fast or hard like it was with the others. I rock slowly over him, grinding my clit on his pelvis. His hands circle my hips, not pushing or squeezing, instead simply connecting us while I control the pace.

In the corner of my vision, Leo and Smitty cuddle together as they watch us. But all my focus is on the alpha under me. Austin. My Austin. Gods, I missed these men so much while they were gone, but it seems the love never faded. We've all grown up, yet somehow our connection is now even stronger. I'm content with the way it all played out, because now that we aren't dumb kids, I can trust our feelings are real. There won't be any silly games or growing pains that young lovers sometimes have. No, this is everything I've ever wanted. I wouldn't change a thing.

I pick up the pace, lifting off Austin's cock until just the tip is still in my pussy, then drop my weight so I sink back down on his shaft. His grip tightens a little and his hips thrust up to meet my strokes, pushing his cock even deeper.

"I'm so close, bug. Please, I'm not sure how much longer I'll last. Your pussy is what dreams are made of." Austin slides a hand from my waist to put his thumb against my clit, rubbing circles right where I need him. Bourbon and warm vanilla meld with my honeysuckle and apricot to make an absolutely decadent combination. Our breathing gets shallow as we near the peak together.

"Bite me, bug," Austin exclaims, surprising me. I thought he'd want to bite me first, but he's giving me the power to claim him from the start. I lock my gaze with his, seeing nothing but sincerity shining in the depths. He gives me a soft smile. "I need you."

As I fall forward to kiss him, he grips my ass and grinds me hard against him as he works his knot into me. I lick and nip my way along his jaw to his pec, then sink my teeth in right above his heart. He cries out and pushes his knot into me fully, hot ropes of cum painting my walls as he locks us together. I release my bite and he pulls me up, aiming for the same spot on my breast. The final connection snaps into place and I come harder than ever before, the pleasure from my new mates ricocheting through the bonds like lightning. My vision starts to go black, but I manage not to pass out.

Austin rolls us to our sides after he tends to his mark, snuggling me into his chest and resting his chin on my head. Leo and Smitty crawl to us, settling in on either side. Smitty spoons me from behind, while Leo cuddles up to Austin's back. He throws his arm over Austin so he can rest it on my side. All my mates are now touching me in some way, and the bonds settle. Now, instead of fizzing and zinging like popping candy, they simply warm me like hot tea on a rainy day.

I drift off to sleep, surrounded by my pack—my *scent-matched* pack—and dream of our future together.

EPILOGUE
1 YEAR LATER

Daisy

"What's this?" I ask Leo when he puts a shoebox on the kitchen island and slides it toward me. A mischievous grin is plastered on his face—which is pretty normal, to be honest, but still makes me suspicious when he's giving me a random box without elaborating.

"Just open it." He encourages sweetly, rocking back on his heels like an excited little boy. Definitely not reducing my suspicions any. It doesn't look like a valentines day gift, the box is unwrapped and looks a little worse for wear.

Keeping it as far away from me as I can, I hesitantly lift off the lid, half expecting something to jump out at me or explode. None of that happens, and when I look inside, I see a bunch of pink envelopes. Just like the ones the pack used to send me before they came home.

"More letters?" I ask Leo, pulling out a handful and setting them on the marble countertop.

"These are the ones we wrote but never sent you." Leo starts to explain, but before he can continue, Austin and Smitty walk into the kitchen. They freeze when they see the open box.

49

"Leo," Smitty says cautiously. "Please tell me that's not what I think it is." His face has gone crimson and now I'm even more intrigued as to what the hell is in these letters.

My curiosity gets the better of me and I pick a letter off the top of the small pile I'd pulled out, opening it before Austin can nab it from my fingers. I read the first few lines and it's instantly clear why they didn't send me these letters.

Daisy girl,

I thought of you today. I mean, I think about you every day, but today I had a particularly nice fantasy while in the shower.

Do you still insist on taking showers with water hotter than lava? You'd come out in your tiny towel, skin hot pink from the temperature of the spray. Your hair would still be wet and tiny rivulets of water would drip down your skin. Oh how I want to trace each of those droplets with my tongue.

Better yet, I want to shower with you. Save water, shower together, right? I'm totally just being eco conscious. I'd help you wash your long black hair, then every inch of your delectable body. Afterwards, maybe you'd let me push you against the cold tile wall while I wrapped that hair around my fist and took you from behind.

Don't worry, Daisy girl. I'd make sure to aim the shower head right at you so you stayed under the warm spray. Nothing but comfort for my girl.

Although... I could take the shower head down and change the setting to a hard pulse. I bet you'd love if I held you tight against me and aimed that water jet right at your clit as I fucked you. You'd squirm until you came all over my cock and then—"

"Leo!" I stop reading when the letter gets even more explicit. "What... I..." Speechless. I'm legitimately speechless. What do I even say about these? I look at my other two alphas. "Did all of you put letters in here, or..."

Smitty's face gets even more red, if that were possible, and Austin hangs his head in shame before looking at me pleadingly. "I'll always be honest with you, bug. Yeah, we all have some of, uh, *those* letters in there." He clears his throat and looks away. "We missed you and occasionally got carried away. Usually we'd satisfy our sexual needs with each other, but sometimes nothing would sate that itch but thoughts of you."

"We didn't think you'd appreciate getting these in the mail out of the blue." Smitty tacks on.

I bite my lip in contemplation before deciding to read another one. This one is from Smitty.

> My Flower,
>   Austin is an evil, evil alpha. He edged the fuck out of me today, using thoughts of you to do it. He painted vivid pictures of us taking you over and over again, sometimes all together. Would you let us do that, flower? Would you let us fuck both those tight holes and fill you with our cum? Maybe you'd like it if Leo fucked you, while I fucked him? Or what if—"

I stop reading again and whip my gaze up to the alpha who wrote this filthy letter with a gasp. He holds his hands up in a placating gesture. "Please don't be mad at us, flower. We're only men, after all."

Scrubbing my hand down my face to hide my flush, I glance at Austin. Despite the incredulity I'm throwing at my alphas, my clit is throbbing and I'm leaking slick. Austin gives a resigned sigh, cards through the letters, and plucks one out. He hands it to me and takes a couple steps back.

> Bug,
>   I found a hiking trail today that you'd love. Not necessarily the hiking part, but the destination. It led to a small waterfall hidden in a copse of trees. There was a calm pool at the bottom surrounded by large rocks and those little purple flowers you like that I can never remember the

name of.

Remember we used to sneak out to go skinny dipping in the lake behind the old stone mill? What I wouldn't give to do that with you again now that we're older. I can clearly imagine you stripping out of your sundress, the moon reflecting off your pale skin before you'd squeal and crash into the water. I want to chase you. Catch you. Make you mine under that moonlight.

I want to make you moan with my fingers, mouth, cock. Bend you over a rock and take you hard and fast. Fuck you softly in a bed of those sweet flowers surrounded by fireflies. Watch Smitty or Leo make you come undone in our own little oasis.

I want you so godsdamn badly, bug. Will you let me have you?

Fuck. I want that, too. All of it. I squeeze my thighs together and can tell the moment my alphas scent my arousal. Their heads snap up, nostrils flaring, low growls starting in their throats. My breathing is faster than usual as I place the letter down and stand from the barstool. Aiming for nonchalance—though not entirely sure I achieve it—I calmly walk out of the kitchen. I can feel my pack's anxiety through the bond, but I need a head start.

When I reach the front door, I smile as I yank it open and call out casually over my shoulder, "It looks like a beautiful day for a swim!"

I take off, laughing as three sets of thundering footsteps scramble after me.

ABOUT THE AUTHOR

Clover Holloway is the cozier side of Unfortunate Reads, writing steamy monster and omegaverse romance that will make you swoon and sweat.

A long time romance reader turned author, she just can't help but make her stories cozy. She's an ADHD agent of chaos so her book topics may vary wildly, but you can always expect an HEA. She's an avid fan of traditional millennial customs including craft breweries, monstera plants, and skinny jeans.

Get lucky at cloverholloway.com.

ALSO BY CLOVER HOLLOWAY

Welcome to Bone Town

Adventure Omegaverse co-written with Thea Masen

Knot Letting Go

Olympic Omegaverse co-written with Thea Masen

Unwrapping the Pack

Part of the Omegaverse Holiday Quickies series

Bubbles with the Pack

Part of the Omegaverse Holiday Quickies series

Slip into Me

A short eel-shifter, fated mates novella.

Originally published in the Strange Love charity anthology.

Taking a Tumble

Meet cute with a dad-bod demon pet shop owner and a curvy,
confident human woman.

Part of the Ghostlight Falls series.

Zero to 69

A sentient object shifter romance co-written with Thea Masen &
Kate McDarris